Alligator Smiling in the Sawgrass

IRA IRONMONGER

Alligator Smiling in the Sawgrass

With Illustrations by Sandra Davidson

YOUNG SCOTT BOOKS · NEW YORK

Library of Congress Catalog Card No. 65-12583

TEXT © 1965 BY IRA IRONMONGER. ILLUSTRATIONS © 1965 BY SANDRA DAVIDSON.

It was a quiet day for the great green alligator in the sawgrass swamp. The sky was that blue blue which means the most perfect of all days, serene weather, contentment. The sun was shining, and the sweetest breeze in the world blew softly.

For a hundred miles there was mostly water, dark green water, and sawgrass. It was indeed an alligator's heaven.

In the very middle of this sawgrass swamp, the green alligator was switching his great tail. Then he gave a turn and heaved around to sun the other side. His eyes almost closed, and he seemed completely and thoroughly relaxed, except--except for one thing. He was smiling. And oh, what a smile that was, the smile of all smiles, so big, so smug, so cunning, so knowing and secret. It made others feel that their world was ridiculous and that the alligator's world was the real and only one.

The alligator in the sawgrass relaxed more and more, but he was looking, too. Out of the corner of his almost-closed eyes, he saw a turtle.

The turtle climbed cautiously out of the water onto the black muck of a smooth bank and settled himself quietly in the sun, turning his head, watching, watching. And then as the sun relaxed him more and more, he sank blissfully on his belly and started stretching his legs way out in the air—stretch, stretch, stretch—like crazy antennas from a round dome shell.

The alligator opened his eye and smiled. But the turtle saw the alligator and quickly slipped into the water and swam away.

The alligator dozed, almost asleep but not quite, for just then he saw a green frog on a pickerel leaf. The frog's eye was solid gold, or so it seemed, and golden stripes spread back from his head like parts of a shining armor. What a beauty he was with the sun shining on him—as if he had dipped into a treasure of molten gold and carried this gold plating forever.

Little by little the alligator's eye opened, his smile deepened, and his sharp teeth were plain to see.

The frog saw the alligator, his gold faded, and he leaped into the water and swam away.

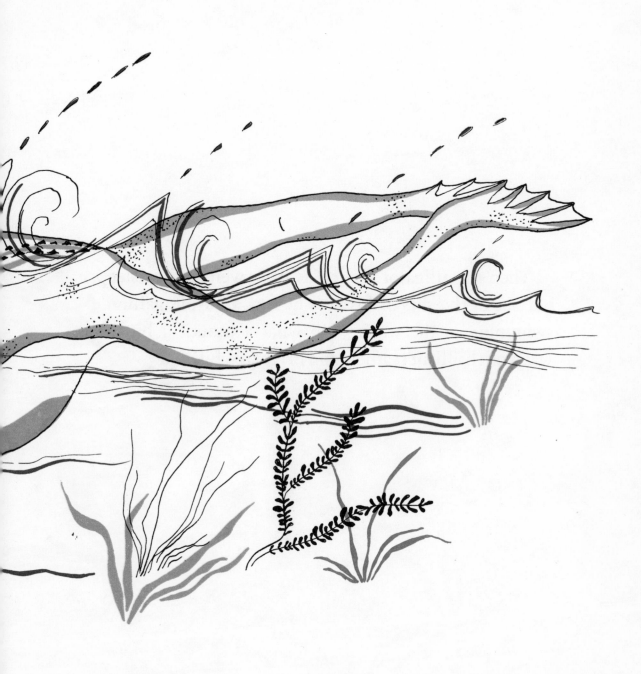

Then the alligator looked as if he were really asleep, but out of the slits of his eyes he saw a purple gallinule swimming in the water. Oh, what a beautiful bird he was, with brilliant feathers and bright red bill.

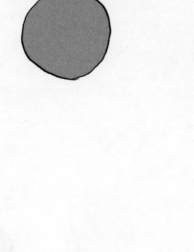

The alligator smiled greedily, a toothy smile.
But the purple gallinule spied the alligator and flew
away in a low flight.

Now a time came when there were no rains. No rains and still no rains. This lasted so long that the water started to dry up and disappear. The black muck became brown and cracked and dry. And still no rains.

The animals of the swamp were nearly dead with thirst, for water is one thing that all animals need even more than food.

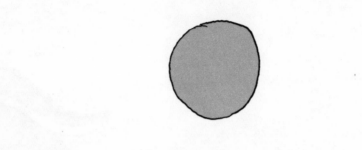
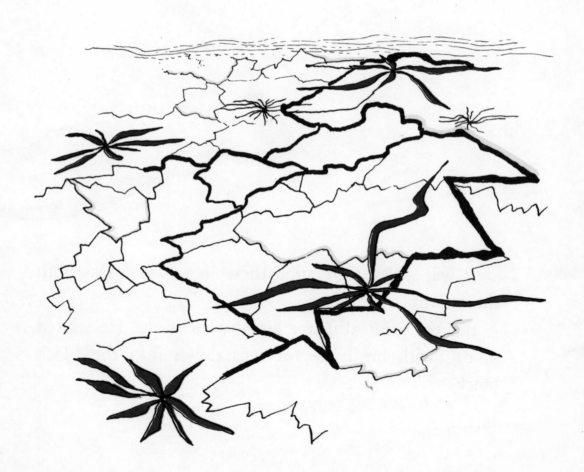

It was a desperate time there in the sawgrass with the swamp so dry.

But the great alligator knew what to do. He started to dig with his powerful legs down into the black muck.

He dug and he dug until he made a hole so deep
that water seeped into it, and he took a long drink.
Then he lay by his water hole, smiling.

The thirsty frog saw the water, and he came and sat very still not far from the alligator.

The parched turtle saw the water, and he, too, came and sat still, near the frog and the alligator.

The purple gallinule, thirsty, came too, and stood near the water hole, quietly preening his feathers.

The alligator smiled, but he did not move.

"If I take a drink, will you eat me?" asked the frog.

"If I take a drink, will you eat me?" asked the turtle.

"Or me?" asked the gallinule.

But the alligator only smiled his wicked smile.

So the frog and the turtle and the gallinule went away, still thirsty.

The next day still no rains came, and the frog and the turtle and the gallinule came to the alligator's hole again, hoping to drink. But the alligator still lay there smiling.

Finally the frog said to the alligator, "Let's be friends."

"Yes," said the turtle, "I like you and want to be your friend, too."

The purple gallinule also said, "Yes, let's all be friends. I like you, too." And the gallinule quietly preened his feathers.

Then slowly the alligator turned to the turtle with his wicked wavy smile, and his jaws opened, cavernous and many-toothed, and as the turtle looked up at the great sharp teeth, his heart almost stopped and he even forgot to pull his head under his shell. But just then...

...the frog skipped in front of the turtle and spoke, surprising everybody.

"Friend!" he said to the alligator.

Yes, that's what the frog said.

And as the alligator looked at this tender, green green frog with the gorgeous golden eye, and as his smile got wider and his teeth seemed to get bigger, the turtle and the purple gallinule slipped into the water hole to drink. But the frog stood still and closed the sheath of gold over one eye, and the other eye almost popped out with all that feeling a green green frog would have at such a moment; and then, then . . .

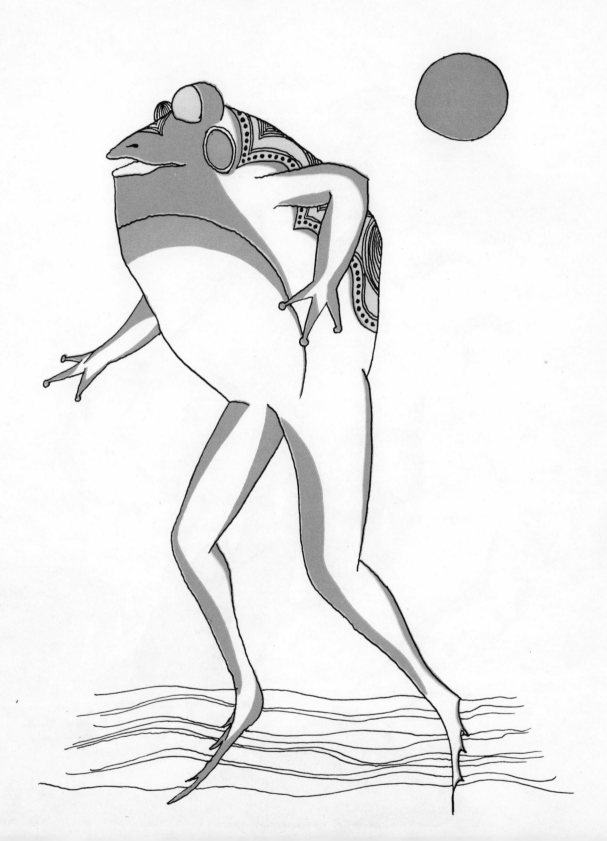

... then the purple gallinule, who had just taken his *first* drink, stepped in front of the frog and said "Friend!"

That's what the gallinule said as he stepped forward on his yellow feet and faced the alligator.

Well, now the alligator was really smiling, as wicked a smile as ever he did smile, and his great jaws and pink throat and big sharp teeth were terrible to see. And as he moved closer to the gallinule, whose brilliant purple-blue feathers and bright red bill made him look so beautiful and so desirable, the frog and the turtle slipped into the water hole to drink. The alligator opened his jaws, wider and wider and wider, and then, then...

...then the turtle, who had just taken his *second* drink, stepped in front of the gallinule and said "Friend!"

And as the alligator looked at the turtle, the purple gallinule and the frog slipped into the water hole to drink. Then the alligator opened his jaws wider and moved closer and closer toward the turtle, but just then...

...then the frog, who was no longer so thirsty, stepped in front of the turtle, looked the alligator right in the eye, and said "Friend!"

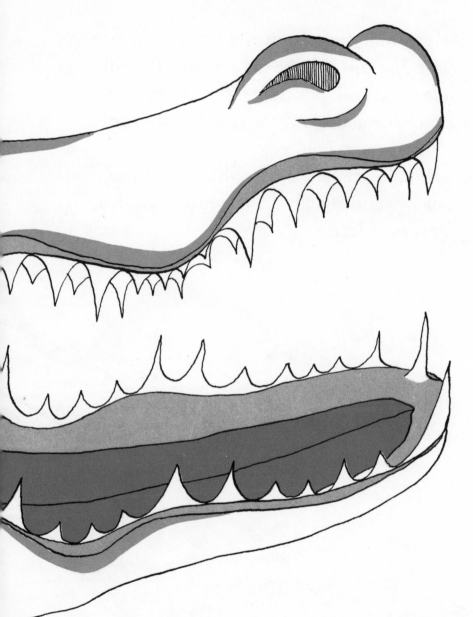

The alligator's eyes seemed to expand with greediness and his smile grew fiercer as he moved closer and closer to the frog. Then...

...then the gallinule stepped in front of the frog to face the alligator. But this time he did *not* say "Friend!"

The gallinule stood still, preening his feathers, and as the wind began to rise and blow, the frog and the turtle went away as fast as they could go.

Now the gallinule was left alone with the alligator. He preened quietly, until finally he loosened a feather, a brilliant purple-blue feather.

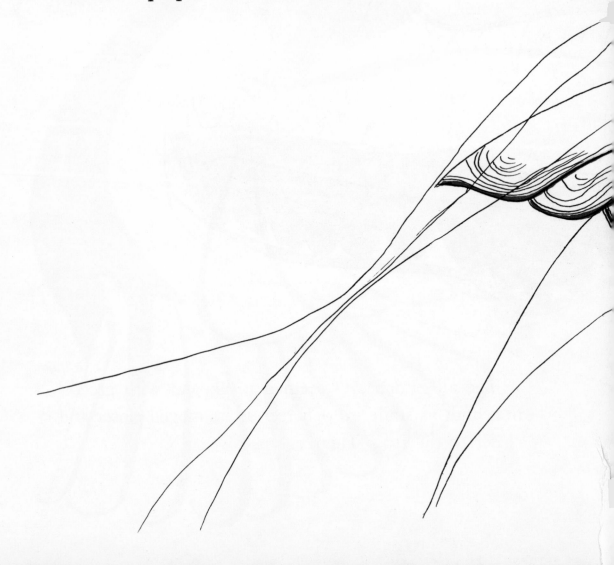

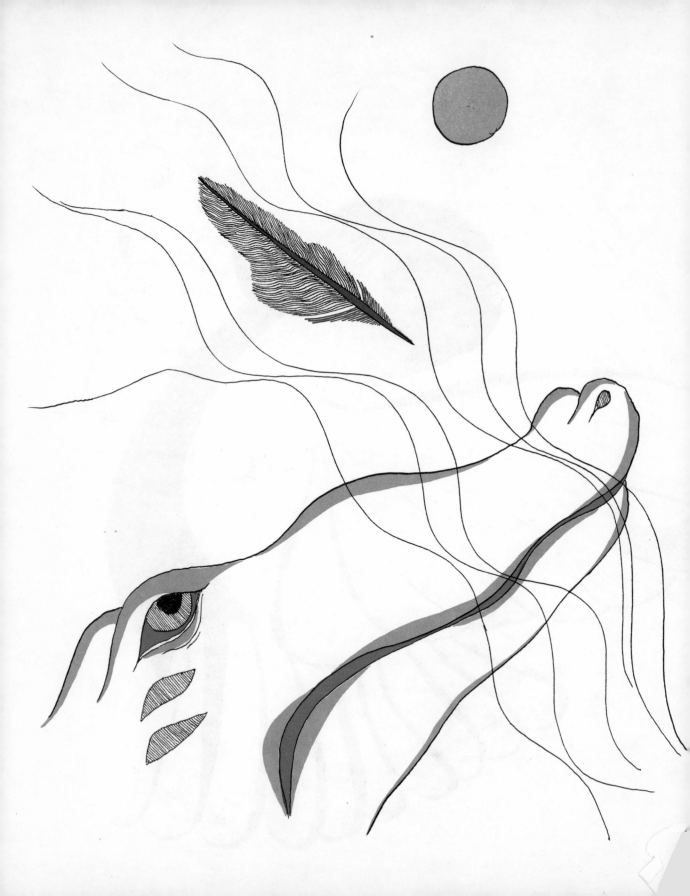

Then the wind came and wafted the bright purple-blue feather ever so lightly until it danced just in front of the alligator's eye.

The alligator looked up, startled at the flying purple-blue feather, and for a moment he stopped smiling.

Away flew the purple gallinule to join his friends in a safe and hidden place.

The alligator was left alone by his pool in the sawgrass.

Then the wind rose higher, and the sky grew dark, and across the sawgrass came a moving sound, like no other sound in the world. And the rains came, and it rained and it rained, until there was plenty of water for all the thirsty animals living in the sawgrass.

Then the sun came out, and it was a happy time in the sawgrass swamp again. And in a pond deep in the sawgrass the frog sat on a pickerel leaf and smiled a gorgeous smile of green and gold, and the turtle and the gallinule smiled with him.

And each was smiling a smile so big, so smug, so knowing and secret, that had the alligator been there to see, it would have made him feel that his private world was ridiculous and that the world of the three friends was the real and only one.

The End